영어로 읽는 세계명작
Story House

THE WIZARD OF OZ

9 오즈의 마법사

L. Frank Baum

WorldCom Edu

Adapted by **Lori Olcott**
Illustrated by **Hong Hee-Kyoung**

Copyright © WorldCom Edu 2006

Published in Korea in 2006 by WorldCom Edu

Printed and distributed by WorldCom Edu

작가와 작품

세계적으로 유명한 미국 작가이자 극작가인 바움 (L. Frank Baum)은 1856년 뉴욕의 치터냉고 에서 태어나 1919년 할리우드에서 생을 마쳤다. 프랭크 바움이 『위대한 오즈의 마법사』를 발표한 것은 1900년으로, 발간 즉시 베스트셀러가 되었으 며, 1939년 MGM사에서 제작한 뮤지컬 영화 『오즈의 마법사(The Wizard of Oz)』는 20세기 최고의 영화로 선정되기도 했다. 이후에도 비 공식적으로 시리즈물이 꾸준히 발간되고 있다.

『오즈(Oz)』는 아름답고 이상한 것, 혹은 환상적인 동화의 나라를 연 상시키는 보통명사로 인식될 정도로 막강한 영향력을 발휘하고 있다.

작품 설명

소녀 도로시는 회오리바람에 휘말려 가게 된 오즈라는 마법의 나라에서 세 친구들을 만나게 된다. 이 제각각의 등장인물들이 자신의 이상과 목 표를 찾아 여행을 떠나면서 겪는 이야기이다. 이 책은 100년이 지난 지 금까지도 그 열기가 식지 않고 있는 가운데 1902년 연극 무대에 오른 것을 시작으로 전세계 곳곳에서 연극이나 영화, 뮤지컬로 만들어지고 있을 정도로 우리에게 친숙한 작품이다.

Introduction

Hello, and thank you for your interest in Worldcom's Story House! I hope you and your children enjoy the stories and characters we present to you here.

These Fairy tales have been passed down from parent to child for generations and generations. They usually teach a lesson. They teach the values that are important in every culture; like being kind, generous and helpful to others. They show that looks can be deceiving. Something beautiful, can be cruel and evil. But something ugly, can be good and loving. They also teach the value of patience. Rewards for good deeds don't always come quickly. But be patient, and the good deeds you do will bring good deeds to you. And if you keep working hard, your efforts will pay off.

I have tried my best to re-tell these stories in modern and natural English, without being too complicated or too hard. Most middle school children can read these stories. But I hope that parents and other adults will enjoy reading these books with their children too. There are interesting parts in each story. I hope there is enough that everyone will enjoy reading the story and listening to the native speakers.

Again, thank you for joining us in Story House. We hope you enjoy your stay.

이 책을 펴내며

안녕하세요. 월드컴의 Story House에 오신 것을 환영합니다. 부디 여러분과 여러분의 자녀들이 이 책이 들려주는 이야기들을 만끽하시길 바랍니다.

이 동화들은 부모에서 아이들에게로 여러 세대에 걸쳐 전해내려 온 이야기로서 교훈을 담고 있습니다. 이웃에게 친절하고 서로 도우면서 아낌없이 베푸는 것, 이러한 가치관의 중요성을 일깨워 주죠. 이러한 것들은 때때로 반대로 표현되기도 합니다. 겉보기에는 아름답지만 잔인하고 사악할 수 있으며, 비록 흉칙하게 보여도 착하고 사랑을 베푸는 사람일 수 있다는 것입니다. 이러한 이야기들은 우리에게 인내의 가치를 일깨워 주기도 합니다. 선한 행동의 대가는 그 즉시 되돌아오지 않습니다. 그러나 참고 기다린다면, 여러분의 선한 행동은 보답을 받을 것입니다. 그리고 열심히 노력한다면 그에 상응하는 결과를 얻을 것입니다.

저는 이 이야기들을 너무 복잡하거나 어렵지 않도록 현대적이고 자연스러운 영어로 전달하기 위해 최선을 다했습니다. 이 책은 중학교 수준의 학생이라면 누구든지 읽을 수 있습니다. 그러나 부모님을 비롯한 모든 이들이 자녀분들과 함께 이 책을 즐길 수 있기를 바랍니다. 이야기마다 제각기 재미있는 부분들이 있습니다. 네이티브들이 들려주는 생생한 이야기는 현장감을 더해 주어 자신도 모르는 사이에 동화세계에 빠져들게 될 것임을 믿어 의심치 않습니다.

다시 한 번 저희 Story House에 오신 것을 감사드리며, 계속 많은 사랑 부탁드립니다.

Lori Olcott

등장인물 주요 등장 인물

도로시
친구 하나 없이 외롭게 지내던 어느 날 세찬 회오리 바람에 휩쓸려
자신이 가장 아끼는 강아지 토토와 함께 마법의 나라로 가게 된다.

허수아비
지푸라기로 만들어진 머리가 아닌, 생각할 수 있는 두뇌(지혜)를
얻었으면 하는 바램을 가지고 도로시와의 여행에 동참하게 된다.

양철 나무꾼
몸이 양철로 되어 있어 따뜻한 마음(심장)을 얻기 위해 도로시와
함께 여행을 떠나게 된다.

사자
자신을 겁쟁이라고 생각하며, 용기를 얻기 위해 도로시와 여행을
함께 한다.

오즈의 마법사
오즈나라의 마법사로 도로시 일행의 소원을 들어주는 조건으로
서쪽 마녀에게서 마법의 빗자루를 가져오도록 시킨다.

마녀
서쪽나라의 사악한 마녀. 빗자루와 마법의 모자로 날으는 원숭이
들을 조종하여 도로시 일행을 자신의 노예로 삼으려 한다.

🌸 그 외의 등장 인물

도로시의 삼촌과 숙모

먼치킨들

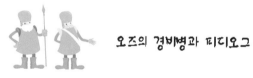

오즈의 경비병과 띠띠오그

날으는 원숭이들

Contents

SH·09·C
MP3

Chapter 1

Once upon a time, there was a young girl named Dorothy. She lived on a farm in Kansas with her Uncle Henry and Aunt Em. She also had a little dog named Toto. Dorothy loved her family, but she did not like Kansas.

once upon a time 옛날에
young 젊은, 어린
name …라고 부르다
live on …에서 살다
farm 농장
Kansas (미국 중부의 주)캔사스
uncle 아저씨, 삼촌

aunt 아주머니, 숙모
also 또한, 역시
little 조그만, 작은
dog 개
family 가족
like 좋아하다

Once upon a time, there was a young girl named Dorothy.
옛날에 도로시라고 하는 어린 소녀가 살았습니다.

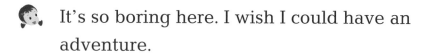 It's so boring here. I wish I could have an adventure.

Nonsense, child. Kansas is a wonderful place.

You don't need adventures. Now go and get the eggs from the henhouse.

Dorothy went to get the eggs from the henhouse.

boring 따분한, 지루한
wish 바라다, …라면 좋은데
adventure 모험
nonsense 허튼 소리
child 아이
wonderful 멋진, 훌륭한

place 장소, 곳
need 필요하다
go(-went-gone) 가다
get 가져오다
egg 달걀
henhouse 닭장

I wish I could have an adventure.
모험을 할 수 있으면 좋으련만.

Now go and get the eggs from the henhouse.
자, 가서 닭장에 있는 달걀이나 가져오렴.

But when she went outside, she saw a big black cloud that touched the ground. It was a tornado!

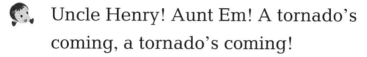 Uncle Henry! Aunt Em! A tornado's coming, a tornado's coming!

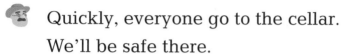 Quickly, everyone go to the cellar. We'll be safe there.

outside 밖에[으로]	ground 땅
see(-saw-seen) 보다	tornado 회오리바람
big 커다란, 큰	quickly 재빨리
black 검은, 시커먼	everyone 모두
cloud 구름	cellar 지하실
touch 접촉하다, 만지다	safe 안전한

---

she saw a big black cloud that touched the ground.
도로시는 땅에 닿아 있는 커다란 먹구름을 보았습니다.
We'll be safe there.
그곳이라면 우린 안전할 거야.

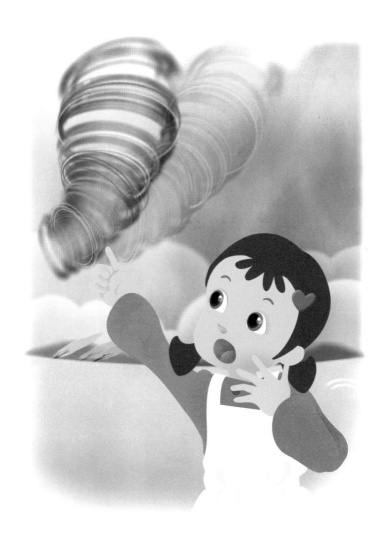

 Wait! Toto is missing. I have to find Toto.

Dorothy ran back to the house to find her dog.

 Toto! Toto! Where are you? There you are, you silly dog. Let's go to the cellar with Uncle Henry and Aunt Em. Oh, no! The house is moving!

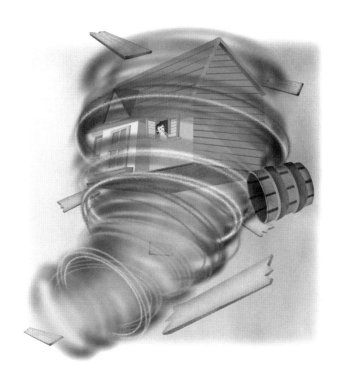

wait 잠깐, 기다려요
missing 없어진, 행방불명인
have to …해야 한다
find 찾다
run(-ran-run) back to
　… 로 다시 달려가다

where 어디에
silly 어리석은, 바보 같은
let's …하자
house 집
moving 움직이는, 이동하는

There you are, you silly dog.
여기에 있었구나. 이 바보 같은 강아지야.

The tornado picked up the house and spun it in the air. The house flew around and around. Dorothy was very scared. She held Toto tightly. Finally, the house stopped moving, and everything was quiet. Dorothy opened the door, but she didn't see Uncle Henry's farm outside. She saw a beautiful garden with trees and flowers. She walked outside into the garden.

 Where are we? This doesn't look like Kansas. Everything is so pretty here.

The tornado picked up the house and spun it in the air.
토네이도는 집을 들어올리더니 공중에서 빙글빙글 돌렸습니다.
She walked outside into the garden.
도로시는 정원으로 걸어나갔습니다.
This doesn't look like Kansas.
이 곳은 캔사스처럼 보이지가 않아.

pick up 들어올리다
spin(-spun-spun) 빙빙 돌리다
in the air 공중에서
fly(-flew-flown) around
 이리저리 날다
scared 무서운, 두려운
hold(-held-held) 잡다
tightly 꽉, 세게
finally 마침내, 드디어
stop 멈추다
everything 모든 것
quiet 조용한, 평온한

open 열다
door 문
farm 농장
outside 밖에[으로]
beautiful 아름다운, 멋진
garden 정원
tree 나무
flower 꽃
walk 걷다, 걸어가다
look like ···처럼 보이다
pretty 예쁜, 멋진

Then she saw some people walking up to her. They looked like adults, but they were as small as children. Their clothes were all blue, even their hats and shoes.

Hello and thank you, powerful wizard. We are the Munchkins, and you saved us from the evil witch.

I'm sorry, but I don't understand. I'm not a powerful wizard. I'm just a little girl. My house was caught in a tornado. I didn't save anyone from an evil witch.

people 사람들, 국민
walk up to …에게로 걸어오다
adult 성인
as small as … 만큼 작은
children 어린이
clothes 옷, 의류
even …조차도
thank …에게 감사하다
powerful 힘센, 강력한

wizard 마법사
munchkin 소인, 먼치킨
save 구하다
evil 사악한, 못된
witch 마녀
understand 이해하다
just 단지, 그저 …에 불과하여
catch(-caught-caught) 잡다
anyone 아무도

Then she saw some people walking up to her.
그 때 도로시는 몇몇 사람들이 자기에게로 걸어오는 것을 보았습니다.

My house was caught in a tornado.
저의 집은 회오리 바람에 휩쓸렸어요.

I didn't save anyone from an evil witch.
전 사악한 마녀로부터 어느 누구도 구한 적이 없어요.

Your house landed on the witch and killed her. See?

The Munchkin pointed to the side of the house. Sticking out from under the house were two legs. Suddenly, the witch's body turned into dust and blew away in the wind. Only her two ruby shoes remained.

land on …에 내려앉다

kill 죽이다

point to …을 가리키다

side 측면, 옆구리

stick out from

　…에서 튀어나오다

under …의 밑에

leg 다리

suddenly 갑자기

body 몸, 신체

turn into …으로 변하다

dust 먼지, 흙

blow(-blew-blown) away

　(바람이)…을 날리다

in the wind 바람 속으로

only 단지, 오직

ruby shoes 루비 구두

remain 남다

Sticking out from under the house were two legs.

집 아래로 두 다리가 튀어나와 있었습니다.

Only her two ruby shoes remained.

오직 그녀의 루비 구두만이 남았습니다.

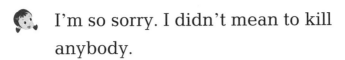 I'm so sorry. I didn't mean to kill anybody.

That's alright. We're happy she's gone. We were all her slaves. Now we are free again. How can we reward you?

I don't need a reward. I just need to get home. My family will miss me.

We can't help you get home. But the Wizard of Oz can. You must go to the Emerald City to see him.

The Emerald City? Where is that?

mean to 진심으로 (…할) 작정이다
kill 죽이다
anybody 아무도
alright 괜찮은
happy 기분 좋은, 행복한
slave 노예
free 자유로운, 석방된

reward …에게 보답하다
get home 집에 가다
miss 그리워하다, 보고 싶어하다
help 돕다
must …해야만 한다
emerald city 에머럴드 시

We're happy she's gone.
우린 마녀가 사라져서 기쁘단다.

We can't help you get home.
우리는 네가 집에 가는 것을 도와줄 수가 없어.

Just follow this yellow brick road. It will take you straight there.

 Here, take the witch's shoes. They are magic shoes, and they will help you.

 Thank you so much. Good bye.

 Good bye, and take care.

The Munchkins waved good bye as Dorothy and Toto walked down the yellow brick road. It was a beautiful day, and the walk was easy.

follow 뒤따르다
yellow 노란
brick 벽돌
road 길, 도로
take 데려가다, 가져가다
straight 곧장, 곧바로
magic 마술

take care 몸조심하다
wave 손을 흔들다
good bye 작별인사
walk down …을 따라 걸어가다
beautiful (날씨가)화창한
walk 오솔길, 걷다
easy 쉬운, 편안한

It will take you straight there.
이 길로 가면 곧장 그 곳이 나올 거야.

The Munchkins waved good bye as Dorothy and Toto walked down the yellow brick road.
도로시와 토토가 노란 벽돌길을 따라 걸어갈 때 먼치킨 사람들은 작별 인사로 손을 흔들어 주었습니다.

Comprehension

Checkup I

I **True or False**

1. Dorothy lived on a farm.

2. The Munchkins were very tall.

3. Dorothy's house killed the evil witch.

4. The Munchkins told Dorothy to go to the Emerald City.

5. The Wizard of Oz lived in Kansas.

II **Multiple Choice**

1. **Who did Dorothy live with?**

    a. She lived with her mother and father.

    b. She lived with her aunt and uncle.

    c. She lived with the Munchkins.

2. **What is a tornado?**

    a. A big black cloud that touches the ground

    b. Dorothy's dog

    c. A kind of farm house

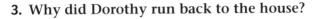
3. Why did Dorothy run back to the house?

    a. To get eggs

    b. To find Toto

    c. To be safe from the tornado

4. What did the Munchkins give to Dorothy?

    a. They gave her some money.

    b. They gave her a beautiful flower.

    c. They gave her magic shoes.

5. Where does the yellow brick road go?

    a. It goes to the Emerald City.

    b. It goes to Kansas.

    c. It goes to Dorothy's house.

Comprehension

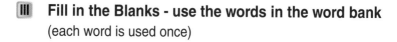

Checkup I

III **Fill in the Blanks - use the words in the word bank**
(each word is used once)

beautiful	clothes	everything	family	free
like	moving	shoes		slaves	walk

1. Dorothy loved her _____, but she did not _____ Kansas.

2. Finally, the house stopped _____, and _____ was quiet.

3. Their _____ were all blue, even their hats and _____.

4. We were all her _____. Now we are _____ again.

5. It was a _____ day, and the _____ was easy.

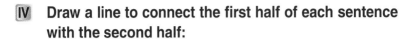

정답은 p.104에

IV **Draw a line to connect the first half of each sentence with the second half:**

A	B

<table>
<tr><td>Dorothy wished for •</td><td>• a little dog.</td></tr>
<tr><td>Toto was •</td><td>• trees and flowers.</td></tr>
<tr><td>Dorothy thought •
Kansas was</td><td>• an adventure.</td></tr>
<tr><td>The beautiful •
garden had</td><td>• dust and blew away.</td></tr>
<tr><td>The witch's body •
turned into</td><td>• a boring place.</td></tr>
</table>

31

Chapter 2

After a while, they came to a cornfield with a low fence around it.

I need a rest, Toto. I guess I'll try on these ruby shoes. Wow! They fit perfectly. And they're so comfortable.

They look very pretty too.

Who said that?

I did. The scarecrow. I'm sorry if I scared you.

after a while 잠시 후에	wow (놀람의 표현)와
come(-came-come) to	fit (옷 등이)꼭 맞다
…에 다다르다	perfectly 딱, 완벽하게
cornfield 옥수수밭	comfortable 편안한
low 낮은	look 보이다
fence 울타리, 담장	pretty 예쁜
around 둘레에, 주변에	who 누구
rest 휴식	say(-said-said) 말하다
guess 생각하다, 추측하다	scarecrow 허수아비
try on 신어 보다, 입어 보다	scare 겁내다, 놀라게 하다

After a while, they came to a cornfield with a low fence around it.
잠시 후에, 그들은 낮은 울타리로 둘러싸인 옥수수밭에 다다랐습니다.

I'm sorry if I scared you.
널 놀라게 했다면 미안해.

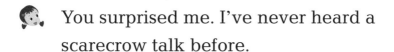 You surprised me. I've never heard a scarecrow talk before.

We don't have much to say. Our heads are stuffed with straw, and we have no brains. I wish I had brains. I want to think great thoughts and dream great dreams. But you can't do that without brains.

I am going to see the Wizard of Oz. Maybe he can help you too.

Do you think so? I would be so happy. Please help me down. I want to go too.

Dorothy helped the Scarecrow get down from his post. Then they walked along the yellow brick road together.

surprise …을 놀라게 하다
hear(-heard-heard) 듣다
talk 말하다
before 이전에
head 머리
stuffed with …으로 채워진
straw 지푸라기
brains 두뇌(지혜)

wish …라면 좋겠다, 바라다
thought 생각
dream 꿈꾸다[목표하다], 꿈[이상]
without … 없이
maybe 아마도
get down from …에서 내리다
post 기둥
walk along …을 따라 걷다

I've never heard a scarecrow talk before.
난 지금까지 허수아비가 말하는 걸 들어본 적이 없어요.

We don't have much to say.
우리는 할 말이 그다지 많지 않아.

Dorothy helped the Scarecrow get down from his post.
도로시는 허수아비가 기둥에서 내려오도록 도와 주었습니다.

A while later, they came to a forest. Standing next to a tree was a metal man with a metal axe.

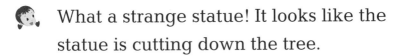 What a strange statue! It looks like the statue is cutting down the tree.

Hrp mr.

Oh, my! The statue is trying to speak.

He's rusted stiff. Here is an oil can. Maybe this will help.

a while later 잠시 후에	statue 동상
forest 숲	look like …처럼 보이다
stand 서다	cut down 베다
next to …의 옆에	Hrp mr(Help me) 도와 주세요
tree 나무	try to …하려고 하다
metal 금속의, 양철의	speak 말하다
axe 도끼	stiff 딱딱하게, 굳어져서
strange 이상한	oil can 기름통

Standing next to a tree was a metal man with a metal axe.

나무 옆에 양철 도끼를 든 양철 인간이 서 있었습니다.

Oh, my! The statue is trying to speak.

오, 이런! 동상이 말을 하려고 하네.

Dorothy and the Scarecrow picked up the oil can and oiled the statue. Soon it began to move its arms and legs. Finally, it could move its mouth to speak.

 Ahh, thank you so much. I got caught in a rain storm and was rusted stiff. I'm the Tin Woodsman. Who are you?

I'm Dorothy, this is my dog Toto, and this is the Scarecrow. We are going to see the Wizard of Oz. I want to go home to Kansas, and the Scarecrow wants brains.

---

pick up 집다, 들다
oil 기름, 기름칠하다
soon 곧
begin(-began-begun) to
　…하기 시작하다
move 움직이다
arms and legs 팔과 다리

finally 마침내, 드디어
mouth 입
get caught in …에 붙들리다
rain storm 폭풍우
tin woodsman 양철 나무꾼
go home 집에 가다
brains 두뇌(지혜)

Finally, it could move its mouth to speak.
마침내, 그 동상은 입을 움직여 말을 할 수가 있었습니다.

I got caught in a rain storm and was rusted stiff.
난 폭풍우를 만나 몸이 뻣뻣하게 녹슬어 버렸어.

Really? Maybe he can give me a heart. A magician made me help him in the forest. But he forgot to give me a heart. I like people who are kind and generous. But you can't be kind and generous without a heart.

 If he can help me, I'm sure he can help you too. Let's go.

So they walked down the yellow brick road together.

really 정말로
maybe 아마도
give 주다
heart 심장, 마음
magician 마법사
make(-made-made) 만들다
help 돕다
forest 숲

forget(-forgot-forgotten) 잊다
people 사람들, 국민
kind 친절한
generous 관대한, 너그러운
without … 없이
walk down … 을 따라 걸어 가다
yellow 노란
brick road 벽돌길

A magician made me to help him in the forest.
한 마술사가 숲에서 자신의 일을 돕도록 하기 위해 날 만들었어.

I like people who are kind and generous.
난 친절하고 너그러운 사람이 좋아.

If he can help me, I'm sure he can help you too.
그가 날 도울 수 있다면, 너도 분명히 도와 줄 수 있을 거야.

Suddenly, a big lion jumped out onto the road. He roared loudly, and showed his big teeth. Dorothy, the Scarecrow and the Tin Woodsman were all scared. But Toto ran up and bit the lion's toe.

Ow, ow! Get it away from me! Get it away!

What's wrong? Toto's only a little dog.

I know, but he scared me.

A little dog scared a big lion like you? You coward.

Yes, I am a coward. I wish I were brave.

suddenly 갑자기
big lion 커다란 사자
jump out 뛰어나오다
roar 으르렁거리다
loudly 큰 소리로, 시끄럽게
show 보이다, 보여 주다
teeth (tooth의 복수형)이빨
scare 겁내다, 놀라게 하다

run(-ran-run) up 뛰어가다
bite(-bit-bitten) 물다
toe 발가락
get ··· away
   ···을 떼 버리다, 제거하다
wrong 잘못된, 틀린
coward 겁쟁이
brave 용감한

A little dog scared a big lion like you?
조그만 개 한 마리가 당신처럼 큰 사자를 위협했다구요?

I wish I were brave.
난 용감해지기를 바래.

Maybe the Wizard of Oz can help you too.

I'm going to ask for a heart, the Scarecrow is going to ask for brains, and Dorothy is going to ask to go home. I'm sure he can give you courage.

Please let me come with you. I'm sorry I scared you.

Yes, you can come with us. But don't roar at us again.

Right. No more roaring.

be going to …할 것이다
ask for 부탁하다, 청하다
go home 집에 가다
courage 용기
come with …와 함께 가다

roar at …에게 으르렁대다
again 다시
right 알았어
no more 더 이상 … 않다

I'm sure he can give you courage.
그는 분명히 너에게 용기를 줄 수 있을 거야.

Please let me come with you.
제발, 너희들과 함께 가게 해 줘.

The new friends continued down the
yellow brick road. Finally, they saw a
green glow over the hills.

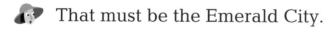 That must be the Emerald City.

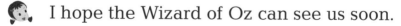 I hope the Wizard of Oz can see us soon.

I hope he won't turn us into frogs.

 I'm sure he's a very nice man. He won't
turn us into frogs.

new 새로운
continue 계속하다
finally 마침내, 드디어
see(-saw-seen) 보다
green 녹색의
glow 빛
over the hills 언덕 너머로

must be …임에 틀림없다
emerald city 에머랄드 시
hope 바라다, 희망하다
soon 곧
turn into … 로 변하다, 바뀌다
frog 개구리
nice 착한, 마음씨 좋은

I hope the Wizard of Oz can see us soon.
오즈의 마법사가 우리를 금방 만날 수 있었으면 좋겠어요.

I hope he won't turn us into frogs.
난 그가 우리를 개구리로 만들어 버리지 않기를 바래.

Soon they came to the city gates. The gates were green as emeralds. A guard met them at the door. His clothes were all green like the gates.

Can I help you?

Yes, sir. We're here to see the Wizard of Oz.

You want to see the Wizard? Please wait a moment.

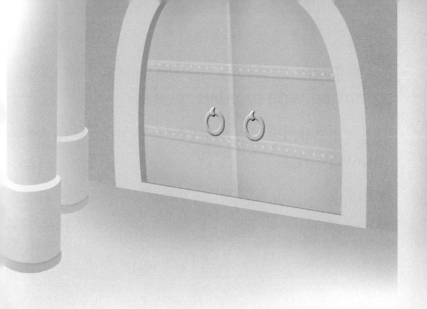

come(-came-come) to
　…에 오다
gate　대문, 큰 문
green as　…처럼 녹색의
guard　문지기, 경비 병

meet(-met-met)　맞이 하다
door　문
clothes　옷, 의류
like　…처럼
wait a moment　잠시 기다리다

His clothes were all green like the gates.

그의 옷은 대문 색깔처럼 온통 초록색이었습니다.

We're here to see the Wizard of Oz.

저희는 오즈의 마법사님를 뵙기 위해 이 곳에 왔어요.

The guard went inside the gates. Soon he returned with another man.

This is Mr. Piddywog. He will take you to the Wizard.

Please follow me.

Excuse me, Mr. Piddywog. Will the Wizard be able to see us soon?

The Wizard is a very busy man. But I think he will be able to see you today.

Will he turn us into frogs?

If you make him angry, he might.

go(-went-gone) 가다
inside 안으로
return with ...와 함께 돌아오다
another 또 다른
take(-took-taken) 데려 가다
follow 따라 오다[가다]

excuse me 실례합니다
be able to ...할 수 있다
busy 바쁜
today 오늘
turn into ...으로 변하다
angry 화난

He will take you to the Wizard.
그가 여러분을 마법사님께 안내해 줄 것입니다.

Will the Wizard be able to see us soon?
마법사님께서 저희를 바로 만나 주실 수 있을까요?

If you make him angry, he might.
만약 당신이 그를 화나게 하면, 그럴지도 모르죠.

Mr. Piddywog took them to a huge castle. Everything in the castle was green. The floors and walls were green marble. The curtains were green silk. Even the windows had green glass. They went through a big green door into a large room. Sitting on a throne in the room was a tall man. He was the Wizard of Oz.

huge 거대한
castle 성
everything 모든 것
floor 바닥
wall 벽
marble 대리석
curtain 커튼
silk 실크, 비단
even …조차도

window 창문
glass 유리(컵)
through …을 지나서
large room 커다란 방
sit on …에 앉다
throne 왕좌
tall 키가 큰
man 남자, 인간

They went through a big green door into a large room.
그들은 큰 녹색문을 지나 커다란 방으로 들어갔습니다.

Sitting on a throne in the room was a tall man.
방의 왕좌에는 키 큰 사람이 앉아 있었습니다.

Hello, good people. How can I help you?

Hello, sir. My name is Dorothy. My house was picked up by a tornado, and I want to go home to Kansas. Can you help me?

I am a Scarecrow, but I want to think great thoughts. Can you give me brains?

I am a Tin Woodsman, but I have no heart. Can you give me a heart?

I am a big, strong lion, but I am a coward. Can you give me courage?

---

good people 선량한 사람들
how 어떻게
pick up 들어올리다
tornado 회오리바람, 선풍
think 생각하다
great thoughts 멋진 생각

give 주다
brains 두뇌(지혜)
heart 심장, 마음
strong 힘센
coward 겁쟁이
courage 용기

My house was picked up by a tornado.

회오리 바람이 저의 집을 들어올렸어요.

I want to think great thoughts.

저는 훌륭한 생각(지혜로운 생각)들을 하고 싶습니다.

Yes, I can do all those things. But first, you must do something for me. In the west lives a Wicked Witch. Her broom has very powerful magic. Bring me her broom, and I will grant your wishes. But be careful. She is very evil, and she will try to make you her slaves. Will you try to get her broom for me?

 I really want to go home. All right, we'll get her broom for you.

 Wonderful! But now it is late. Mr. Piddywog will show you some rooms. You may sleep here tonight. Tomorrow, you will go west to find the Wicked Witch's broom.

all those things 그 모든 것들
first 먼저, 우선
something 어떤 일[것]
west 서쪽(으로)
live 살다
wicked witch 사악한 마녀
broom 빗자루
powerful 강력한
magic 마술
bring 가져오다

grant (들어)주다, 수여하다
wish 바램, 소원
careful 조심하는
slave 노예
wonderful 멋진, 훌륭한
late (때가)늦은, 지각한
may …해도 좋다
sleep 잠자다
tonight 오늘 밤
tomorrow 내일

In the west lives a Wicked Witch.
서쪽에는 사악한 마녀가 살고 있다.

she will try to make you her slaves.
마녀는 너희들을 자신의 노예로 삼으려 할 것이다.

Comprehension

I True or False

1. Dorothy met the Scarecrow in a rice field.
2. The Tin Woodsman was made by a magician.
3. Toto scared the Cowardly Lion.
4. Everything in the Emerald City was green.
5. The Wizard of Oz turned the Cowardly Lion into a frog.

II Multiple Choice

1. How did Dorothy's magic shoes fit?
   a. They were too small.
   b. They were too big.
   c. They fit her perfectly.

2. How did the Tin Woodsman get rusted stiff?
   a. He got caught in a rain storm.
   b. He fell into a lake.
   c. Someone poured oil on him.

3. Who bit the Cowardly Lion's toe?

   a. Dorothy did.

   b. Toto did.

   c. A bug did.

4. How many new friends did Dorothy meet on the yellow brick road?

   a. She met two new friends.

   b. She met three new friends.

   c. She met four new friends.

5. Where did the Wicked Witch live?

   a. She lived in the west.

   b. She lived in the east.

   c. She lived in the Emerald City.

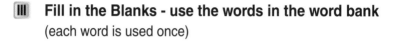

III Fill in the Blanks - use the words in the word bank
(each word is used once)

castle	down	dream	evil	hope
make	statue	think	took	turn

1. I want to _____ great thoughts and _____ great dreams.

2. It looks like the _____ is cutting _____ the tree.

3. I _____ he won't _____ us into frogs.

4. Mr. Piddywog _____ them to a huge _____.

5. She is very _____, and she will try to _____ you her slaves.

정답은 p.105에

IV **Draw a line to connect the first half of each sentence with the second half:**

A	**B**
Dorothy wants •	• a heart.
The Scarecrow wants •	• the Wicked Witch's broom.
The Tin Woodsman wants •	• a brain.
The Cowardly Lion wants •	• to go home.
The Wizard of Oz wants •	• courage.

SH-09-C
MP3

Chapter 3

The next morning, Dorothy, the Scarecrow, the Tin Woodsman and the Cowardly Lion all met at the gates of the Emerald City. They turned west and started to look for the Wicked Witch's castle. But the Wicked Witch had very powerful magic. Her eyes could see anywhere in her kingdom. As soon as Dorothy and her friends crossed the border, the Wicked Witch saw them.

next morning 다음 날 아침
meet(-met-met) 만나다
gate 대문
turn west 서쪽으로 향하다
start to …하기 시작하다
look for …을 찾다
eyes 눈

anywhere 어디든지
kingdom 왕국
as soon as …하자 마자
cross 건너다
border 국경
see(-saw-seen) 보다

———————●———————

They turned west and started to look for the Wicked Witch's castle. 그들은 서쪽으로 향했습니다. 그리고 사악한 마녀의 성을 찾기 시작했습니다.

Her eyes could see anywhere in her kingdom.
마녀의 눈은 그녀의 왕국 어디든지 볼 수가 있었습니다.

Who are these people? I think the Wizard of Oz sent them. I will make them my slaves. Flying Monkeys, come to me!

Quickly, a group of monkeys flew down to the Wicked Witch. They all had wings like giant eagles.

There are some strangers from the Emerald City in my kingdom. Catch them and bring them to my castle.

Yes, my Queen.

send(-sent-sent) 보내다   like …처럼
flying monkeys 날으는 원숭이들   giant eagle 거대한 독수리
quickly 재빨리   stranger 낯선 사람, 이방인
a group of 한 무리의   catch 붙잡다
fly(-flew-flown) 날다   bring 데려오다
wing 날개   queen 여왕

———•———

They all had wings like giant eagles.
그들은 모두 커다란 독수리처럼 날개를 달고 있었습니다.

There are some strangers from the Emerald City in my kingdom.
내 왕국에 에메랄드 시에서 온 낯선 무리들이 있다.

The monkeys flew up and away. Soon they saw Dorothy and her friends. They zoomed down and picked them up high into the air. When they landed, they put everyone into a cold, dark room. Dorothy started to cry.

 This is terrible. We've been caught. Now none of us will get our wishes.

 There, there, Dorothy. It's alright. We're still together. I'm sure we'll be ok.

The Tin Woodsman gave Dorothy a hug and let her cry on his shoulder. Her tears rusted his arm stiff, but he didn't mind.

———————○———————

We've been caught. 우린 잡히고 말았어요.

Now none of us will get our wishes.
이제 아무도 소원을 이루지 못할 거예요.

Her tears rusted his arm stiff, but he didn't mind.
그녀의 눈물이 그의 팔을 뻣뻣이 녹슬게 했지만, 그는 개의치 않았습니다.

fly away 날아 가다
zoom down 급하 강하 다
pick up 들어 올리 다
high into the air 공중 높이
land 육지에 닿다
put into …에 놓다
everyone 모두, 전부
cold 추운, 차가운
dark 어두운, 컴컴한
start to …하기 시작하다

catch(-caught-caught) 붙잡다
none of 아무도 …않다
wish 소망, 바램
still 여전히, 아직도
hug 껴안음, 포옹
shoulder 어깨
tear 눈물
rust 녹슬게 하다
stiff 뻣뻣하게, 굳어져서
mind 신경 쓰다

A while later, the Flying Monkeys returned. They took everyone to the Wicked Witch. Dorothy was very scared, but she tried to be brave.

Who are you people? What are you doing in my kingdom?

Hello, ma'am. The Wizard of Oz sent us. May we please have your broom?

My broom? You want my broom? Of course not! It's my broom. And now you are my slaves.

a while later 얼마 후에
return 돌아오다
take(-took-taken) 데리고 가다
scared 무서운, 두려운
try to …하려고 애쓰다
brave 용감한

kingdom 왕국
ma'am (호칭)부인, 아주머니
send(-sent-sent) 보내다
broom 빗자루
of course not 물론 아니다
slave 노예

They took everyone to the Wicked Witch.
날으는 원숭이들은 일행 모두를 사악한 마녀에게로 데리고 갔습니다.

May we please have your broom?
저희가 당신의 빗자루를 가져도 되나요?

The Cowardly Lion had an idea. He would scare the Wicked Witch, and then take her broom. He raised his long claws, showed his big teeth, and roared at the Wicked Witch. She waved her broom at the Lion. Suddenly, he was frozen like a statue.

 You thought you could scare me? Hah! Now I have a new lion statue. I will put you by my front door. But I will need another statue for the other side of my front door.

have(-had-had) (생각이)나다
idea 생각
scare 놀라게 하다, 겁주다
raise 들어 올리다
long 기다란
claw 발톱
show 보이다
big teeth 큰 이빨
roar at ...에게 으르렁대다

wave 흔들다
suddenly 갑자기
frozen 얼어 붙은
like a statue 동상처럼
think(-thought-thought)
　생각하다
front door 정문
another 또 하나의, 다른
other side 다른 쪽, 맞은편

You thought you could scare me?
네가 날 겁줄 수 있다고 생각했느냐?

But I will need another statue for the other side of my front door.
하지만, 정문 맞은편에 쓸 또 하나의 동상이 필요하겠구나.

She waved her broom again, and a bucket of water appeared.

This water will rust the Tin Woodsman. He will be my other statue. And you, Scarecrow. I will use your straw for my fire place!

The Wicked Witch waved her broom a third time. The Scarecrow's arm burst into flames. Dorothy grabbed the bucket of water and threw it on the Scarecrow. The water put out the fire, but it also splashed on the Wicked Witch.

---

a bucket of water
한 양동이의 물
appear 나타나다
other statue 다른 동상
use 사용하다
straw 지푸라기
fire place 벽난로
third time 세 번

burst into 별안간 …하기 시작하다
flames 불꽃, 화염
grab 잡다
throw(-threw-thrown) 던지다
put out (불을)끄다
fire 불
splash on …에 튀기다

I will use your straw for my fire place!

네 몸의 지푸라기를 내 벽난로에 써야겠다!

The Scarecrow's arm burst into flames.

허수아비의 팔에 불이 확 타올랐습니다.

 Oh no! What have you done? You got me wet!

I'm sorry, but the Scarecrow's arm was on fire. I had to put it out. I didn't mean to splash you too.

You terrible child. I'm melting! I'm melting!

It was true. She was melting like an ice cream cone. Soon, there was nothing left but her hat and her broom.

do(-did-done) 하다
get(-got-gotten) …하게 하다
wet 젖은
on fire 불타서, 불이 나서
have(-had-had) to …해야 한다
mean to 진심으로 …할 작정이다
terrible child 못된 아이
melt 녹다

true 사실인, 틀림없는
ice cream cone 아이스크림콘
soon 곧
nothing 아무것도 …않다
left 남아 있는
but …이외에는
hat 모자
broom 빗자루

What have you done? You got me wet!
너 대체 무슨 짓을 한 거냐? 날 젖게 했어!

I didn't mean to splash you too.
당신에게 물을 튀기게 할 생각은 추호도 없었어요.

Soon, there was nothing left but her hat and her broom.
곧, 마녀의 모자와 빗자루 외에는 아무것도 남지 않았습니다.

When she was gone, all her spells broke. Suddenly, the Lion could move again. The Flying Monkeys flew down to see what happened.

She's dead. The Wicked Witch is dead.

I'm so sorry. It was an accident. I didn't know water would hurt her.

This is wonderful. She was an evil witch. We're glad she's gone.

But now we don't have a queen any more. Who will rule us?

What are you talking about?

---

go(-went-gone) 가다, 사라지다
spell (마술의)주문
break(-broke-broken) 깨지다
suddenly 갑자기
move 움직이다
fly(-flew-flown) 날다
happen 일어나다, 발생하다

dead 죽은
accident 사고, 사건
hurt 다치게 하다
evil 사악한, 못된
not any more 이제[더 이상]…않다
rule 지배하다, 다스리다
talk about …에 대해 말하다

The Flying Monkeys flew down to see what happened.

날으는 윈숭이들은 무슨 일이 일어났는지 보려고 아래로 내려왔습니다.

I didn't know water would hurt her.

전 물이 그녀를 해칠 줄은 미처 몰랐어요.

But now we don't have a queen any more.

그렇지만 이제 우리에게 더 이상 여왕은 없어.

The Wicked Witch had the magic hat of the Flying Monkeys. Whoever has the magic hat is our ruler, and we have to obey them. You are a nice person. Will you take the magic hat and be our queen? We'll do whatever you say.

No, I can't be your queen. I have to go home to Kansas.

magic 마법의

whoever 누구나

ruler 지배자, 통치자

obey 따르다, 복종하다

person 사람

take 가지다

be ···이 되다

whatever 무엇이든지

say 말하다

go home 집에 가다

Whoever has the magic hat is our ruler, and we have to obey them. 마법 모자를 쓰고 있는 사람은 누구든지 우리의 지배자이고 우리는 그들의 명령에 따라야 해요.

Will you take the magic hat and be our queen?
당신이 마법 모자를 가지고 우리들의 여왕이 되어 주시겠어요?

We'll do whatever you say.
당신이 말하는 것은 무엇이든지 하겠습니다.

I have an idea. We will give the magic hat to the Flying Monkeys. Then they will be their own rulers. No one will ever make them do anything again.

Really? Hooray! We're free!

The Flying Monkeys were very happy. They gave Dorothy the Wicked Witch's broom and carried them back to the Emerald City.

idea 생각
magic hat 마법 모자
no one 아무도 …이 아니다
make …하게 하다
do anything 어떤 일을 하다
again 다시
really 정말로

hooray 만세
free 자유로운, 석방된
happy 행복한, 기분좋은
give(-gave-given) 주다
carry back 다시 옮기다
emerald city 에메랄드 시

No one will ever make them do anything again.
이제 다시는 아무도 그들에게 다시 어떤 일도 시키지 못할 거야.

They gave Dorothy the Wicked Witch's broom and carried them back to the Emerald City.
날으는 윈숭이들은 도로시에게 사악한 마녀의 빗자루를 주었습니다.
그리고 그들을 다시 에메랄드 도시로 데려다 주었습니다.

Comprehension

I   True or False

1. The Flying Monkeys had wings like giant eagles.

2. The Wicked Witch gave Dorothy her broom.

3. The Wicked Witch turned the Scarecrow into a statue.

4. The Flying Monkeys asked Dorothy to be their queen.

5. The Flying Monkeys carried them back to Kansas.

II   Multiple Choice

1. Where did the Flying Monkeys put Dorothy and her friends?

    a. They put them on an old boat.

    b. They put them in a small house.

    c. They put them in a dark room.

2. How did Dorothy feel when she met the Wicked Witch?

    a. She was scared.

    b. She was happy.

    c. She was angry.

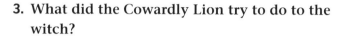

정답은 p.106에

3. **What did the Cowardly Lion try to do to the witch?**

   a. He tried to turn her into a statue.

   b. He tried to scare her.

   c. He tried to splash water on her.

4. **What did the water do to the Wicked Witch?**

   a. It gave her a cold.

   b. It rusted her stiff.

   c. It melted her.

5. **What did the Flying Monkeys give to Dorothy?**

   a. They gave her a bucket of water.

   b. They gave her the Wicked Witch's broom.

   c. They gave her wings.

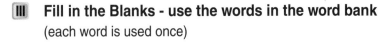

III **Fill in the Blanks - use the words in the word bank**
(each word is used once)

anything	bucket	cry	hat	hug
kingdom	nothing	make	see	threw

1. Her eyes could _____ anywhere in her _____.

2. The Tin Woodsman gave Dorothy a _____ and let her _____ on his shoulder.

3. Dorothy grabbed the _____ of water and _____ it on the Scarecrow.

4. Soon there was _____ left but her _____ and her broom.

5. No one will ever _____ them do _____ again.

IV **Draw a line to connect the first half of each sentence with the second half:**

A	B
The Wicked Witch •	• broke when the Witch was gone.
The Flying Monkeys •	• had very powerful magic.
Dorothy's tears •	• burst into flames.
The Scarecrow's arm •	• rusted the Tin Woodsman's arm.
All the Wicked Witch's spells •	• caught Dorothy and her friends.

Chapter 4

Soon, everyone was back in the throne room. The Wizard of Oz was waiting for them.

soon 곧, 머지않아   throne room 왕실
everyone 모두   wait for …을 기다리다
back 돌아온

———————●———————

Soon, everyone was back in the throne room.
머지않아, 그들 모두는 왕실로 돌아왔습니다.

Thank you for the Wicked Witch's broom. And now I will help you. But I really don't need to. You already have everything you want.

Scarecrow, you wanted brains. But you had the idea to give the Flying Monkeys the magic hat. This was a very smart idea. Tin Woodsman, you wanted a heart. But you made Dorothy feel better when she was scared. You must have a big heart to help someone like that.

Cowardly Lion, you wanted courage. But you tried to scare the Wicked Witch. Only a very brave person would try to do that. You made your own wishes come true.

help 돕다	make(-made-made)
need to …할 필요가 있다	…하게 하다
already 이미, 벌써	feel better 더 나아지다
everything 모든 것	courage 용기
brains 두뇌(지혜)	brave 용감한
idea 생각	person 사람
smart 똑똑한	one's wish 소원, 바램
heart 심장, 마음	come true 실현되다

───────○───────

You already have everything you want.
너희들은 이미 너희들이 원하는 모든 것을 가지고 있다.

But you made Dorothy feel better when she was scared. You must
have a big heart to help someone like that.
하지만 넌 도로시가 무서워할 때 마음을 편하게 해 주었다. 그처럼 사람을
돕는 것은 네가 분명히 큰 심장(넓은 마음)을 가졌다는 증거다.

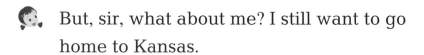 But, sir, what about me? I still want to go home to Kansas.

Dorothy and Toto, you can go home any time you want to. Your ruby shoes have the magic to take you anywhere. Just tell them where you want to go.

I can go home now? That's wonderful. But I will miss my new friends. Good bye, Scarecrow. I hope you think many great thoughts.

Good bye, Dorothy. I'll miss you too. But my brains know you'll be happy at home.

sir (경칭)마법사님
what about …은 어떻게 되나요
any time 언제든지
ruby shoes 루비 구두
magic 마법
anywhere 어디든지

just 그냥, 단지
tell 말하다
miss 그리워하다
new friends 새로운 친구들
great thoughts 멋진 생각들

———————○———————

Your ruby shoes have the magic to take you anywhere.
네 루비 구두는 널 어디든지 데려다 줄 수 있는 마법을 갖고 있느니라.

But my brains know you'll be happy at home.
하지만 내 머리는 네가 집에 가면 행복할 것이란 걸 알고 있단다.

Good bye, Tin Woodsman. I hope you will be kind and generous to many people.

Good bye, Dorothy. My heart is sad to see you go. But I know you miss your aunt and uncle too.

Good bye, Lion. I hope you will protect your forest as bravely as you protected me.

Good bye, Dorothy. I'm afraid we'll never see you again. Remember us. We'll remember you.

My heart is sad to see you go.
내 마음은 널 떠나보내야 하는 것이 슬퍼.

I hope you will protect your forest as bravely as you protected me.
당신이 절 보호해 준 것처럼 당신의 숲도 용맹하게 지켜주길 바래요.

kind 친절한
generous 마음씨 좋은, 관대한
many people 많은 사람들
sad 슬픈
aunt 숙모, 아주머니
uncle 삼촌, 아저씨

protect 보호하다, 지키다
forest 숲
as bravely as …처럼 용감하게
afraid …이라고 생각하다
never 앞으로 …않다
remember 기억하다

Thank you for your help, Wizard. I'm ready to go home now.

 First, close your eyes and think about home. Then click your heels together three times. Then say, There's no place like home.

 There's no place like home.

ready to ···할 준비가 된	together 함께
first 먼저, 우선	three times 세 번, 세 차례
close one's eyes 눈을 감다	say 말하다
think about ···에 대해 생각하다	place 장소, 곳
heels 발뒤꿈치	

Then click your heels together three times.
그리고 나서 네 발뒤꿈치를 세 번 부딪쳐라.
There's no place like home.
세상에 집 만한 곳은 없다.

Dorothy felt a soft wind on her face. When she opened her eyes, she was back on her uncle's farm.

Toto, it worked. We're home again. Uncle Henry, Aunt Em, where are you?

Dorothy, is that you? Where were you, child?

We could not find you after the tornado. I'm so glad you're safe.

That tornado was some adventure.

Yes, it was. I've had enough adventures for a while. I'm glad to be home again.

feel(-felt-felt) …을 느끼다
soft 부드러운
wind 바람
face 얼굴
open one's eyes 눈을 뜨다
back 돌아온
farm 농장
work 작용하다, 효과가 있다
where 어디에

child 어린이, 아이
find 찾다
after …한 후에
tornado 회오리바람, 선풍
safe 안전한
adventure 모험
have(-had-had) 가지다
enough 충분한
for a while 잠시, 얼마 동안

We could not find you after the tornado.
우린 회오리 바람이 지나간 후에 널 찾을 수가 없었단다.

I've had enough adventures for a while.
전 얼마 동안 충분한 모험을 했어요.

Dorothy was happy on her uncle's farm.
But she always remembered her good
friends in the Land of Oz.

happy 행복한, 즐거운   good 좋은
always 항상, 늘   friend 친구
remember 기억하다

Dorothy was happy on her uncle's farm.
도로시는 삼촌의 농장에서 지내는 것이 즐거웠습니다.

Comprehension

Checkup IV

I True or False

1. The Wizard thought the Cowardly Lion was very brave.

2. Dorothy did not want to go home anymore.

3. Dorothy's friends went to Kansas with her.

4. Uncle Henry and Aunt Em knew where Dorothy was after the tornado.

5. Dorothy was glad to be home again.

II Multiple Choice

1. Who was waiting for Dorothy and her friends?

    a. Mr. Piddywog was waiting for them.

    b. The Wizard of Oz was waiting for them.

    c. Uncle Henry and Aunt Em were waiting for them.

2. What did the Wizard think about the Scarecrow's idea?

    a. He thought it was a brave idea.

    b. He thought it was a bad idea.

    c. He thought it was a smart idea.

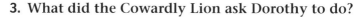

3. What did the Cowardly Lion ask Dorothy to do?

    a. He asked her to remember them.

    b. He asked her to think great thoughts.

    c. He asked her protect his forest.

4. How did Dorothy get home?

    a. She followed the yellow brick road.

    b. She used the ruby shoes.

    c. She flew in another tornado.

5. Who did Dorothy see on the farm?

    a. She saw her aunt and uncle.

    b. She saw her friends in the Land of Oz.

    c. She saw the Flying Monkeys.

Comprehension
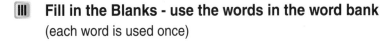

Checkup IV

III **Fill in the Blanks - use the words in the word bank**
(each word is used once)

about	enough	eyes	happy	heart
know	someone	true	while	wishes

1. You must have a big _____ to help _____ like that.

2. You made your own _____ come _____.

3. My brains _____ you'll be _____ at home.

4. First, close your _____ and think _____ home.

5. I've had _____ adventures for a _____.

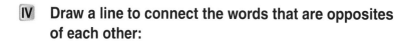

정답은 p.107에

IV Draw a line to connect the words that are opposites of each other:

A				B

A

Kind •

Friends •

Cowardly •

Slave •

Adult •

B

• Free

• Brave

• Child

• Strangers

• Wicked

ANSWERs

Comprehension Checkup

Checkup I (28~31p)

I   **1.** T   **2.** F   **3.** T   **4.** T   **5.** F

II   **1.** b   **2.** a   **3.** b   **4.** c   **5.** a

III   **1.** family, like   **2.** moving, everything
     3. clothes, shoes   **4.** slaves, free
     5. beautiful, walk

A	B
IV Dorothy wished for	a little dog.
Toto was	trees and flowers.
Dorothy thought Kansas was	an adventure.
The beautiful garden had	dust and blew away.
The witch's body turned into	a boring place.

Comprehension Checkup

Checkup II (58~61p)

I   **1.** F   **2.** T   **3.** T   **4.** T   **5.** F

II **1.** c   **2.** a   **3.** b   **4.** b   **5.** a

III **1.** think, dream   **2.** statue, down
       3. hope, turn   **4.** took, castle
       5. evil, make

	A	B
IV	Dorothy wants	a heart.
	The Scarecrow wants	the Wicked Witch's broom.
	The Tin Woodsman wants	a brain.
	The Cowardly Lion wants	to go home.
	The Wizard of Oz wants	courage.

Comprehension Checkup

Checkup III (82~85p)

I   **1.** T   **2.** F   **3.** F   **4.** T   **5.** F

II   **1.** c   **2.** a   **3.** b   **4.** c   **5.** b

III   **1.** see, kingdom   **2.** hug, cry
        3. bucket, threw   **4.** nothing, hat
        5. make, anything

	A	B
IV	The Wicked Witch	broke when the Witch was gone.
	The Flying Monkeys	had very powerful magic.
	Dorothy's tears	burst into flames.
	The Scarecrow's arm	rusted the Tin Woodsman's arm.
	All the Wicked Witch's spells	caught Dorothy and her friends.

Comprehension Checkup

Checkup IV (100~103p)

I   **1.** T   **2.** F   **3.** F   **4.** F   **5.** T

II   **1.** b   **2.** c   **3.** a   **4.** b   **5.** a

III   **1.** heart, someone   **2.** wishes, true
         3. know, happy   **4.** eyes, about
         5. enough, while

A	B

IV
Kind — Strangers
Friends — Wicked
Cowardly — Brave
Slave — Free
Adult — Child

Word List

다음은 이 책에 나오는 단어와 숙어를 수록한 것입니다.
* 표는 중학교 영어 교육 과정의 기본 어휘입니다.

E

F

G

Notes

Notes

Notes

Story House
09. The Wizard Of OZ 오즈의 마법사

펴낸이   임 병 업

펴낸곳   (주)월드컴 에듀

등록   2000년 1월 17일

주소   서울특별시 강남구 언주로 120

인스토피아 빌딩 912호

전화   02)3273-4300(대표)

팩스   02)3273-4303

홈페이지   www.wcbooks.co.kr

이메일   wc4300@wcbooks.co.kr